THE LIBRARY OF
UNREQUITED LOVE

THE LIBRARY OF UNREQUITED LOVE

SOPHIE DIVRY

*Translated from
the French by*

Siân Reynolds

MacLehose Press
New York • London

MacLehose Press
An imprint of Quercus
New York • London

Copyright © Les Éditions Les Allusifs Montréal (Québec), 2010
English translation copyright © 2013 by Siân Reynolds
First published in the United States by Quercus in 2015

ISBN 978-1-62365-403-0

Library of Congress Control Number: 2015931867

Distributed in the United States and Canada by
Hachette Book Group
1290 Avenue of the Americas
New York, NY 10104

Manufactured in the United States

10 9 8 7 6 5 4 3 2 1

www.quercus.com

To all those men and women who will always find
a place for themselves in a library more easily than
in society, I dedicate this entertainment

Reading is, with friendship, one of the surest contributions to the work of grieving. It helps us, more generally, to grieve for the limitations of our life, the limitations of the human condition

DIDIER ANZIEU, *Le Corps de l'Oeuvre*

WAKE UP! WHAT ARE YOU DOING LYING there? The library doesn't open for another two hours, you shouldn't be here at all. If that isn't the limit! Now they've started locking readers in my basement. Honestly, there's no end to what I have to put up with. No, no point shouting, it's not *my* fault . . . But I know who *you* are, you know your way around the library. You mooch around this place all day, so sooner or later you were bound to end up spending the night here. No, don't go away, now that you're here, you can give me a hand. I'm looking for a book they want upstairs. *Existentialism Is a Humanism*, you know, book by Sartre, they've somehow lost it down here, so take a look on the shelves, please. What? You don't recognize me? But I work in this room every day. So I must be completely unnoticeable. Nobody sees me, that's my problem. Even in the street, people bump into me and say, "Oh, sorry, didn't see you."

The invisible woman, that's who I am, the invisible woman, the one in charge of the Geography section. Ah, yes, now you've remembered who I am, of course. Oh there it is, thanks very much, that was quick of you. *Existentialism Is a Humanism* has no business down here in my basement, we don't have philosophy on this level. It suits the eggheads on the ground floor. I'll give it back to them, they'll be pleased, they've been looking for it for ages up there. See, you really are a big help. Anyway, I'm not allowed to open the doors for you, it would mean calling the security people, it's too dangerous. Yes, it is, it's dangerous, because it would be unprecedented, first time ever. And in a library, one should never draw attention to oneself. If you attract attention, you'll disturb people. You can just stay here with me while I get my reading room ready. I have more books to shelve. And since you're so efficient, can you take out of the History section all the geography books that readers have shoved in there? Go on, don't complain: sorting, rearranging, not disturbing people, that's what I do all day long. Taking books off shelves and putting them back on, over and over, ad infinitum. No, it's not that fascinating, sorry about that. Because to put a book back in the right place, I don't even have to look at the author's name. I just have to read the numbers here, on this little label stuck on the spine, and slip it in with the others that have the same shelf mark. There, you see, that's all. And I've been doing this job for twenty-five years now, twenty-five years, with the same rules, it never changes. Even if they call me upstairs to the Loans Desk, it's no better. Checking books in and out, making the bar codes go beep-beep, think that's fulfilling? Beep-beep, "Back on September twenty-sixth, good-bye"; beep-beep, "Back on May fourteenth, thank you." Being a librarian isn't an especially high-level job, I can tell you. Pretty close to being in a factory. I'm a cultural assembly line worker. So what you need to know is, to be a librarian, you have to like the idea of classification, and to be of a docile nature. No initiative, no room for the unexpected; here, everything is in its place, invariably in its place. Did you sleep well, at least, down here? No? You were scared? Oh, but it's very quiet. I like the peace and quiet, I find it reassuring. But that's how I am, I need precision and routine. I could never work in a railway station: too much going on and the very idea that a train was going to be late would give me a panic attack. Anyway, I never take the train nowadays, I'm too old for that. I don't drive either, it's too dangerous and I hate parking lots, I like old-fashioned beauty. Just the very idea of getting on the on-ramp to a highway gives me palpitations. Don't stay standing up like that, I'll get you some coffee. I always bring a Thermos of coffee when I come in early. Drink up, it'll make you feel better. Believe me. Now just sit down there and don't bother me again, or I'll get stressed. Even in small-town libraries like this, people make terrible mistakes in their shelving. It drives me up the wall, it's a sign of how pathetic they are. Not only do they shut absentminded readers into my basement at night, but they shelve the books all wrong as well. Because, theoretically, whether you're in Paris, Marseille, Cahors, Mazamet or Dompierre-sur-Besbre, you ought to be able to find the same book in the same place. See, take a classic work of sociology, Émile Durkheim's *The Division of Labour in Society*. Well, there it is, shelf mark 301. Next to *Suicide*. That's another great classic by Durkheim: *Suicide*. Same author, same shelf mark: 301 DUR. Works every time. Can't go wrong. The man who invented this system, his name was Melvil Dewey. He's our founding father, for all us librarians. Just a little guy from a poor family somewhere in America, and he was only twenty-one when he thought up the most famous classification system in the world. Dewey is the Mendeleev of librarians. Not the Periodic Table of Elements, but the classification of areas of culture. His stroke of genius was to divide up the areas of knowledge under ten broad headings he called "classes": 000 for general works, 100 for philosophy, 200 for religions, 300 for social sciences, 400 for languages, 500 for mathematics, 600 for technology, 700 for fine art, 800 for literature, 900 for history and geography—and everything else they couldn't classify ends up here in the basement too. Yes, sorry, my coffee is always too strong, that way I don't get my colleagues scrounging it off me. Well, Dewey called his system "the Dewey Decimal Classification." Simplicity itself. It was over a century ago. He had a right to be proud of himself: he had methodically arranged all human knowledge. That was important. Because before that, let me tell you, it was completely erratic. They didn't just classify by author, they sometimes put books on the shelf by size, or date of acquisition. Now I come to think of it, the confusion it must have caused. Glad I didn't live then. I couldn't have put up with that kind of anarchy. Already my Geography section, as I was saying, is a sort of dump. They chuck in books on numismatics, military medals, genealogy, psychoanalysis, the occult . . . It's a catch-all category. Which bothers me. I like nice clear-cut categories. See, over there, on the right, that's History. Personally, I like that section, in fact, I love it. But I was appointed to manage Geography and Town Planning, over here on the left. And let me tell you that between Geography and History, that is between the shelf marks 910 and 930, there's a great gulf fixed. A symbolic line, not to be crossed. In fact, History takes up most of the space. It has virtually the whole of the 900s. Oh, I don't hold it against history, because I'm fond of it. But I only get 900 and 910 for me, quite little ones. Not a lot, but just see what Dewey does with them, even if there are only a few books. Incredible. 910: General works of geography. 914: Geography of Europe. Then after the first three figures you put a decimal point, so the more detailed the idea is, the longer the shelf mark. Do you follow? And by the way, please don't drink the whole Thermos. So here we have 914.4: Geography of France. 914.43: Geography of the Île de France region. Next along: 914.436: Geography of Paris. I could go on, nothing slips through the net of this classification. It's infallible. So to sum it up, a shelf mark is between three and six figures long, after that you add the first three letters of the author's name. *Existentialism Is a Humanism* = 194 SAR. If you just remember that, your night will not have been wasted. To know your way around a library is to master the whole of culture, i.e. the whole world. I'm not exaggerating. In any case, it's my belief that Dewey was totally megalomaniac. Well, obsessed at any rate. I'm sure he was one of those people who can't get to sleep unless their slippers are neatly lined up at the foot of the bed and the kitchen sink has been completely scoured. I understand him, I'm the same myself. This was someone who devoted his entire life to libraries, his existence revolved around books, that was it. Since he was American, and you know how practical they are, Dewey set up a cabinet-making firm to manufacture library furniture, the *Library Bureau Company*, pardon my English pronunciation. The company still exists today. Oh, that's so American. It sells really good quality furniture. They have a few pieces in Paris, at the library at Beaubourg, the Pompidou Centre. This library can't afford them, of course,

our furniture is shoddy stuff. I've told the Head
Librarian, and indeed the Mayor, that cheap bookcases aren't good enough, but what can I say, they
couldn't care less. Anyway, I don't count for anything. No one listens to me. I'm totally invisible. In
fact, if I hadn't deliberately made a noise just now
when I arrived, you'd still be fast asleep, you
wouldn't have been disturbed. I'm sorry to have
interrupted your snooze, but perhaps you think it
a matter of little consequence that it was an American who dreamed up the ambitious plan of classifying the whole of human knowledge? Well,
don't be naïve. When that fanatic Dewey classified
literature, he set up a monument of ethnocentrism:
810, American literature; 820, English literature:
two whole divisions for the English-speakers. 830
to 880, European literature: six divisions for the
whole of old Europe. And what about the hundreds of other languages in the world? Just one
division: 890. Just one heading, see? So Dewey's
classification has been modified. They decided it
would be more politically correct to increase the

space for nonaligned countries. O.K., not a bad idea. But then there were more tendentious changes. Graphic novels for instance, they've been taken out of 741.5, because they were crowding out Fine Arts. They get a special section now, near the door. I was against it, I didn't approve of that at all, but well, what did they care? The Religion section, where there are fewer and fewer books, has been tacked on to the end of History—Dewey would have been O.K. with that. But what really gets me, a huge mistake, is moving Languages from 400 to 800. What have they put there instead? Nothing. So shelf mark 400 is now unoccupied, it's just empty. You agree with me, don't you, it's ridiculous. It makes my head spin, having a vacant shelf mark. What's going to be put there? What domain of culture and human knowledge that we haven't properly valued is going to take it over in the future? I prefer not to think about this unoccupied shelf mark, it frightens me. Like swimming far out to sea. I've only done that once, in the days when I was still taking vacations. More than fifteen years ago. Nowadays I don't go on vacation, not even weekends, I can't stand leisure. There's no space for leisure in life. You're either going up or down, end of story. And at a certain point in your life, you have to decide what you want to do with your time. Well, as I was saying, I was younger then. I'd been dragged onto a boat, I was taken sailing, and suddenly they were all in wetsuits and over the side. I jumped in too, because I didn't want to be the only one left on deck. But I wasn't happy, we were out of sight of the coast. And suddenly, thinking how deep it was under my feet, I had a panic attack. Brr, I nearly drowned, it still makes me shiver. Horrible things, vacations! Give me some of that coffee, that'll make me feel better. The idea of leaving an empty shelf mark is so abysmally stupid. It really upsets me. They should never have laid a finger on the Dewey System. Because now, instead of calling it the Dewey Decimal Classification, they call it "the universal classification." That gets people going, I can tell you. Some of my colleagues spend their lives working out tiny nuances in the shelf marks, classifying, numbering, declassifying, de-numbering. And all for the sake of order, hierarchy, tidiness. Oh, don't think I'm complaining. I like my job. Well, O.K., I confess, when I began studying, I didn't mean to become a librarian. I wanted to be a middle school teacher, but I failed the teaching diploma. So now here I am, an assembly line worker, shelving books, issuing them, beep-beep. I'm nobody, nothing at all. But no, no, I'm not complaining. At least I don't have to shout all day at a lot of out-of-control schoolchildren. I have a quiet life. I work here Tuesday to Saturday, ten till five, with a lunch break between one and two. Yes, I agree, the opening hours aren't anywhere near long enough for the readers. But it's no good complaining to me, go and see the Mayor. The rest of the time, I'm at home. I live on the rue Victor Hugo, between the cemetery and Pratier, the butcher's. I live on my own. I'm fine. Nobody bothers me. No, I'm not that old, but I know at my age, my career's pretty much over, so I'm just waiting till I retire and trying not to draw attention to myself. I read a lot. I do what the people upstairs tell me. I say good morning politely to the Head Librarian. I do the necessary. I do get a little bored . . . As for men, I've given up on them. It's just impossible in a place like this, impossible. It's not exactly the sticks, but if you're a sensitive, cultivated soul like me, it's . . . well, it's very provincial. I need wider horizons. So men, no, that's all over. Love, for me, is something I find in books. I read a lot, it's comforting. You're never alone if you live surrounded by books. They lift my spirit. The main thing is to be uplifted. That's why it's particularly painful to have to work in the basement, it's really dark here, don't you think? Architects never think of those of us who have to work down here. Architects never think of anything, in my opinion anyway. I know quite a bit about architects, because I see them regularly poking around in this section. I never offer to help them, no, never. The first architect, or student of architecture, who comes along, with his silly glasses and portfolio, pays the price for the rest of them. They won't get any advice, not a smile, *niet, nada*. I believe in collective punishment. It's only fair. Whoever designed this stuffy basement condemned me, arbitrarily and definitively, to live in a dungeon, so I persecute them all in return. I get my revenge when I make them go up and down to different floors a few times before finding the right book, or when I annoy them with my trolley while they're trying to concentrate on their work, or when I keep trying to open one of their badly designed windows, or turn the air conditioning on or off. I harass them, yes, that's right. Don't look at me with those big eyes, I know when to stop. Nobody notices my little game. And anyway, you can't trust the readers an inch. I don't mean you personally, I'm speaking in general: readers only come into a library to cause mayhem. So if you want to limit the damage, you have to watch them like a hawk. My mission can be reduced to that, yes: stopping the readers from perverting the overall arrangement of my basement. I don't always manage it. They do stupid things all the time. Inevitably. They put the books back in the wrong place, they steal them, they mess them up, they dog-ear them. Some people even tear out pages. Imagine, tearing pages out when photocopies are only seven cents a shot! It's men that do that, every time. And underlining like crazy, that's always men as well. Men just *have* to make their mark on a book, put in their corrections, their opinions. You see the pathetic comments they write in the margin: "Yes!," "No!!!," "Ridiculous," "Very good," "O.T.T.," "Wrong." It's forbidden to write on the books, that's in the Library Rules. You don't remember? Every borrower has to sign the form when they get their reader's ticket, but everyone forgets about it, they don't respect anything. Well, men, readers, are just trouble, trouble period. And since I dislike anarchy, I've drawn my line in the sand. I prefer the company of books. When I'm reading, I'm never alone, I have a conversation with the book. It can be very intimate. Perhaps you know this feeling yourself? The sense that you're having an intellectual exchange with the author, following his or her train of thought, and you can accompany each other for weeks on end. When I'm reading, I can forget everything, sometimes I don't even hear the phone. Not that the phone rings all that often at home, just my mother calling once a week, but if I'm really deep into a book, I don't even hear that. It's a marvelous feeling, very stimulating, but it does call for a minimum of effort. Intellectual effort, I mean. Making an effort has never scared me. And reading my books in silence like that, I'm at peace: my favorite authors are all dead. They're not likely to come along and rearrange my slippers or scribble in the margins. I feel really calm then. Quite calm. Well, to tell the truth, if I can be totally honest with you, there's this boy over there, in the History section, much younger than me, he is. He's doing research, for a thesis, or a diploma, I don't know, something like that. He comes here to study. I watch him. That's all, it doesn't go any further. He's very intelligent.

He's doing some serious research. I only have a Bachelor's degree. Anyway. I was thinking (you have plenty of time to think in this job) and I told myself that I could never fall for someone who was less well educated than me. The men who carry the books from the stacks for us, for instance, they can still make the odd remark to me, well in fact they don't do that so much now, but even when they did, just little remarks or winks, I tell you, I hardly bothered looking at them. Not intellectual enough. To appeal to me, a man can be shorter than me or taller, richer or poorer, older or younger, nothing's an obstacle, I'm open-minded, you see. But he has to be more intelligent. And he has to be clean-shaven, no stubble, I hate scruffy people. My young researcher is very well dressed. His name's Martin. The first time I saw him, I'd just got off the bus at my usual stop, avenue Salengro, and I was walking along the sidewalk toward the new entrance to the library, opposite the little shopping center. At first, I didn't pay any attention, it was just someone walking ahead of me, probably going to the shopping center to work or shop, like all the wasters who join the rat-race to sell, or make, or buy any number of pointless consumer goods that don't contribute in any way to the edification of human knowledge. So, I just saw this young man ahead of me, but I didn't pay any particular attention to him. But as it takes five minutes to get to the wretched entrance now, I went on looking at what I could see, his back, his legs, the nape of his neck. Not that I spend my time looking at young men, not my style, O.K., you agree, but I didn't have anything else to do. Because I don't go around with those headphones bombarding tuneless garbage straight into your brain. Not my cup of tea. Not at all. On the bus, I see all these zombies. One with his iPod, another on his cell phone, number three fiddling with his tablet. None of these morons reads a book on the bus. Never. That would be too much effort. And then you expect them to come around here look-ing for education? No, not a chance, just look at them, brains switched off. As it happened, luckily,

Martin was walking ahead of me without a cell phone or headphones. I noticed that right away. Yes, that was a good point, I admit. I hadn't seen his face yet, but I was already imagining that he had a high forehead, dreamy eyes and a determined mouth. When we reached the market place, he didn't turn off to the shopping center: no, he kept on going toward the library, like me. Then I realized it was the back of his neck that had captivated me, right from the start. Because is there anything more fascinating about a person than a beautiful neck seen from behind? The back of the neck is a promise, summing up the whole person through their most intimate feature. Yes, intimate. It's the part of your body you can never see yourself. A few inches of neck, with a trace of down, exposed to the sky, the back of the head, the last good-bye, the far side of the mind? Well, the back of Martin's neck is all of that. His square shoulders are a perfect setting for the upward sweep of his head, his curly hair caresses those few inches of skin, as if to soften his apparent solidity: a gentle and promising balance, so one already senses the strength of the body and the intelligence of the soul. How I admired him that day. Then, of course, I got to see his face. It's a marvelous face, if a bit severe: I like boys with strong eyebrows, they're reassuring. When he comes in here, Martin sits on this chair. He's right, it's the calmest, quietest corner of the room and you get a bit of natural light. Between us, it's just "good morning," "good evening," nothing else. But I admit, this boy seems to me . . . how shall I put it? Well, it's not really physical, no, he's very polite, and I like that side of him too, but, well, he just seems . . . very intelligent. That's it. And exactly the kind of intelligence that I appreciate. Someone who spends his time reading books, taking notes from books, selecting books, and all that so as to write another book, it's really admirable. At the same time, he's not pretentious, not at all. Very modest. I'd be quite ready to invite him home for a cup of Darjeeling. Why not? He could sit on my sofa. That's what sofas are for: sit down, drink a cup of tea, talk about literature. At least that's how I see it. I'm sure he and I have heaps of things in common, I just sense it. Like me, Martin isn't very high up the hierarchy, he's a foot-soldier of research, another assembly line worker, an anonymous toiler in the vineyard. But alas, I don't dare invite him. I'm afraid I never will have the courage either. I don't want to disturb him in his work. And anyway, he doesn't come all that often, about once a week perhaps. The rest of the time, he must be at the University Library. Well, naturally, a local council library isn't a cultural El Dorado. Mind you, we've done well to get this far: more than two hundred thousand books available to borrow, it might never have happened. To get a public library in a little provincial town like this took centuries. And his highness the Mayor isn't overly fond of us either. We never see him here, in fact, or anyone from his family. So apart from people like you, who are capable of falling asleep in a reading room, who comes here? Not that many people. They're so ungrateful. When you think of all the trouble it took to reach this point. Because if you care to look more closely into the history of libraries, who could have collected all these books so methodically? Not country bumpkins like you, let me tell you. You don't work on a farm, do you? Sorry, thought you did. But anyway, I don't need to see your tax return to see that unlike those kings and monks and nobles, people with power, in short, you wouldn't have been able to collect thousands of books. Take Cardinal Mazarin for instance, seventeenth century: he had forty thousand books in his personal library in Paris. Nice little collection. And one day, he decided to open it to the public. That was pretty good going, for a cardinal. Still, we shouldn't be fooled: what mattered most to him was the prestige it brought him. The building got to be called "the Mazarine." He was as proud as punch, our cardinal. Well, after all, books are like carriages, the whole point is to show off. True culture for rich people doesn't come till later, it creeps up on them, and it's not well regarded. In his case, it took the shape of an admirable man called Gabriel Naudé. A talented little commoner, who started off wanting to be a doctor, but he fell in love with the cardinal's books, so he became his head librarian. When the weather was overcast, you couldn't see a thing inside the poky Mazarine, it was worse than here. But they had an excuse, it was early days. Impressive early days. Gabriel Naudé there and then defined a dozen categories: theology, philosophy, history and so on, and about thirty sub-categories. *Pre-Melvil Dewey*! Which proves the Americans didn't invent anything. Well, isn't an American a European who missed the boat home? I don't go anywhere nowadays, myself. Oh, let's not even mention boats, I'll get a hot flash. Airplanes? Are you kidding? Never! No, I don't go anywhere these days. What's the point, I ask you? You never have enough time to understand what you're seeing, and I can't stand only half knowing things. Trying to visit an art gallery in a couple of hours is stupid. Two hours, that's hardly enough for me to take in a single painting. No, I'm not exaggerating.

Oh, well, perhaps you, when you look at a picture, you're just happy to let your feelings respond to colors arranged in a certain order. That kind of romantic swooning isn't my cup of tea. No, no. I have to have all the possible information, about even the tiniest picture. That's the way I am, I have to know everything; the painter's biography, where his studio was, what were the technical conditions, who commissioned the painting, the political context, the aesthetic quarrels of the day, how the paints were chemically composed—everything. No, I can't stand having just a smattering of superficial knowledge. So tourism, no, out of the question. I used to go to Italy, back in the day. Now I just read the books in the Fine Arts section. I learn more and it costs me less. I'm sure Martin would agree with me about that. A perfectionist, a workaholic, an obsessive. In fact he must be writing a thesis or something. I worked that out when I finally peeped discreetly over his shoulder and managed to read: "Peasant revolts in the Poitiers region in the reign of Louis XV."

Written on the outside of a big blue folder. I assumed that was the subject of his thesis. *"Peasant revolts in the Poitiers region in the reign of Louis XV."* I'd have preferred it if he'd been working on the reign of Louis XVI or the Revolution. Because Louis XV—kind of a nothing reign. Louis XIV or Louis XVI, yes, no problem, but Louis XV is just a black hole. Look under 944.655, and you'll see, we don't have anything. Whereas in 944.75, history of the French Revolution, there's much more. My favorite shelf mark. And there are nine subdivisions in it. You really can't imagine. For instance, 944.755 is the Terror. With that kind of shelf mark, the librarian can have really interesting conversations with the readers. In 1989, the Bicentennial, these books were flying off the shelves. They're lucky, the people in charge of History. Because if you're working in Geography you can wait forever for a reader to ask you to suggest a book for vacation reading . . . "Peasant revolts in the Poitiers region in the reign of Louis XV." Not easy to start a conversation about that. In any case, French history before the Revolution—I might have read about a hundred books on it, but I can't get my head around it. Well, is there anyone who can? Really? Charlemagne a bit, Joan of Arc perhaps, but honestly before the Revolution, nobody actually cares about it. It all seems a very long time ago, all that old stuff. Go on, admit it, I won't blame you. And yet the people who lived in the *ancien régime*, they weren't stupid at all, they respected books, especially after the Renaissance, with the invention of printing, not to mention the reformation and all those monomaniacs with their translations of the Bible, but it was all very elitist. The peasants, the poor, the Third Estate, the public, nobody bothered about them. That's why people like me, from humble backgrounds, we don't feel concerned about anything much before the Revolution. That's how it was. And it could have stayed that way. No movement. Apart from, excuse me while I have a little laugh, a few peasant revolts in the Poitiers region. And then wham! The Revolution. What I admire about our revolutionaries is their capacity for organization. Robespierre was the least head-in-the-clouds person in history. Him and his colleagues, they were quite right to issue all those thousands of laws and decrees and orders. Because it really needed a good cleaning out. Before that it was all privileges, tithes, salt tax, plumed hats. With their holy days for Saint Eustace and Saint Eulalia, different weights and measures in every parish in France, people speaking dialects nobody could understand ten miles away, it was total chaos. And if you were faced with that anarchy, you needed some beautiful, clear and popular rationality. So they went right at it, no dillydallying. My greatest regret is that they gave up on the republican calendar when it was perfectly rational: instead of our fifty-two weeks that never work out the same from year to year, the revolutionaries decided every month would have three ten-day weeks, to be called *décades*, with a day off every *décade*, thirty-six *décades* in the year—plus the metric system, France divided into 80 *départements*, and the kilo at ten times a hundred grams: now that's what I call organization. But these days, are we grateful to Robespierre? Have you ever seen a Robespierre Square or a street named after Saint-Just in France? No? It's a scandal. Yeah, yeah, I know, don't tell me, the guillotine, the Terror, etc. Oh stop, it really annoys me. Basically, Robespierre is everyone's bad guy. Not a good thing to be, the bad guy, it doesn't get you points in the opinion polls. Well, I'd like to see you try. A thousand years of monarchy to get rid of, you needed more than a few wimps to do that job. They weren't going to get anywhere by sitting around being nice, were they? It's only because they *were* bad guys that you're sitting there, you ungrateful cockroach, clodhopper, or whatever you are. No, don't get upset, it's just that when people talk about the guillotine, it gets me worked up. I'm sorry, do sit down. What I mean is, most people don't realize the extent to which the Revolution is the cradle of all ideas in our society. Actually, modern history can be summed up in three major events that altered our view of the world for good: the French Revolution, the bloodbath of the Great War, and the invention of the contraceptive pill. The whole of French history, you've got it there, but I can't explain it all now, it would take too long and I'm not sure you'd be able to appreciate it. But there was one thing they didn't manage to do, in the Revolution. Oh, I don't blame them, they didn't have any computers in those days, but it's the Big Catalog. In 1789, they confiscated twelve million books from the aristocrats and the clergy, and they thought they'd distribute them to public libraries. That's a terrific idea. You have to give them that. Admit it. Thank you, I'm glad you agree. But alas, if you want to know the rest, they never got around to it. Too much going on, a crisis, not enough money. Then the morons under the Directory couldn't be bothered. Too much trouble. And what really annoys me is that Napoleon could have started the project going again, but that show-off was too busy bringing total mayhem to the whole of Europe. That's another reason I don't go traveling. Napoleon's always been there first. I can't stand it. And when I say total mayhem, I'm being polite. In fact, he destroyed everything: looted, burned, pillaged. Who was the real gravedigger of the Revolution? Napoleon. A barbarian and a tyrant. Encouraging the people to read wasn't what he was about, he preferred to get a whole generation of young men massacred marching through the snow. Did you know that the Napoleonic wars killed more Frenchmen than the First World War? No, of course not. You don't learn stuff like that on T.V., you learn it here, by reading the history periodicals we subscribe to. A barbarian, that's what he was, a dictator. When I see the number of books that come out every year about that uncivilized little runt, I can't understand the fascination with Napoleon, it's appalling, I just don't get it. And we have this nice periodicals room, very comfortable. But I'm probably talking too much. I wouldn't dare go on like this to Martin. That's where I'm contradictory: I like men who are more intelligent than me, but

the idea that they might think I'm stupid para-
lyzes me. And I might have read a hundred or
more books on the Revolution, I still don't know
everything about it either. So where was I? Oh yes,
after that, came Louis-Philippe, who was a lot
more democratic than he gets credit for, and he
would have liked every region to have a library.
But it didn't happen. That's no reason to be unfair
about Louis-Philippe, he wasn't that bad. And I
like a man with sideburns. I think Martin would
be even better looking if he had sideburns.
Although it was his intelligence that first attracted
me, I still allow myself to imagine: ah, Martin with
sideburns. Well. Anyway. Now the Third Repub-
lic *did* try to make books available to everyone,
but the First World War didn't help. It was total
chaos. The filth, the trenches, the mud, the blood,
the barbed wire. What a nightmare, you have to
say. The guillotine was much more civilized. A
heart-breaker, the Great War, what a step back-
ward for humanity, shelf mark 944.855. Durkheim lost his son to it and his young disciples, a

terrible disaster for science. That's the way it is: wars always kill the sons, never the fathers who made the decisions. And once we got ourselves out of that mess, the libraries were in a terrible state. Completely underdeveloped: hardly any books on loan, no heating, not enough places to sit. If you were a big shot, they'd allow you to enter these shrines to knowledge, but no way were they going to let *hoi polloi* in. They "segmented" the public, as they would say today. Cemeteries full of books, that's what the librarians were in charge of, not living places. And even here, even now, it's no good my putting out comfortable chairs or trying to make the lighting more attractive, it's not really a welcoming environment. Not to mention the people upstairs, who do all they can to stop my little initiatives. Even today, two hundred years after Robespierre, a library is still a bit of a gloomy place. Oh, don't try and tell me different. Listen, you might meet someone on the way to the movie theater, or the restaurant, or the swimming pool, or a café, looking happy, that's normal. But have you ever heard people in the street saying things like: "I'm going to spend the day in the library, yippee!" "Oh, fantastic, you lucky thing!" And we might have stayed forever in that lamentable condition, if there hadn't been this one man who got up one morning and said No! And that was Eugène Morel. You won't have heard of him, of course. Eugène Morel's entirely forgotten today. If any of us human primates can go and educate ourselves in nice, friendly, light-filled libraries, it's because of him. This young man did a survey of libraries in Europe and the United States and published it in 1908. Absolute bolt of lightning. The old librarians who trained at the École des Chartes didn't like his book. Not at all. Well, he didn't beat around the bush, Morel, he had a clear set of demands: make it easier to borrow books, have longer opening hours, keep the collections up to date, have comfortable seats, special areas for children, and the underpinning of the whole thing, the ideal, the supreme aim, was that *the people* should be able to read. What do you mean, there's no need to shout? I'm not shouting, I'm being enthusiastic, it's not the same thing. It's true, I'm a big fan of Eugène Morel. Know why? Because he used to say: "Libraries have one enemy worse than the archivist, and that's the architect." Oh, I really like that, pithy, to the point, brilliant, that's my boy, Eugène. But it wasn't until after the Liberation in '44 that things really changed. From then on, they started to take some notice of the people. The Americans, who looked down on us while they were showering us with money, wanted to tell us all about public libraries. But at that point we said: "Stop! We've read Eugène Morel, we know exactly what to do, thanks." You'll have to forgive me. I come from a very ordinary background, so I know exactly what I owe and who I owe it to, I was the first person in my family to get as far as the *baccalauréat*. So you can't fool me. In the 1970s, when I started work, it was all still going full blast. People had the ideal of public service in those days. Not like now, with the youth who go straight to the comic book shelves, they don't see me, they don't even bother to reply when I say good morning. Then we had the socialists in power in 1981, and all that. But, excuse me, we didn't have to wait for them to roll up either, before getting the library at Beaubourg, the Pompidou Centre. Open every night till 10:00 p.m. So people *could* have read books. If they could be bothered. Because, if I'm allowed a personal view, even though librarians are supposed to be politically neutral and welcome everyone, whatever their views, I've lost my illusions about "the people" and the socialists. And I don't even believe in the State much these days. Yes, I'm a public servant, but I ask you, do revolutions ever start with public employees? In any case, it was our ancestors who did everything, before us. Our job now is to do all we can to live up to the standards they set us. With all their books around us. Don't you ever tell yourself that? How are we ever going to live up to the people who went before us, how will we not let them down? Well, I do. And it distresses me. Terribly. Don't tell me you never feel distress. Everyone does, it's part of life. Even great writers feel it, in fact especially them. Take Simone de Beauvoir, she had terrible bouts of depression. Poor thing, I can sympathize. And Durkheim, the sociologist. Completely neurotic. At the end of his life he had insomnia, nervous spasms, anguish. He died of a broken heart after the Great War. I get anxiety attacks too. It doesn't always show, I can control myself, you know, but, oh yes, I do suffer. The worst thing is getting these compulsive obsessions. They're always at me. I just have to see a book shoved in the wrong way on a shelf, sticking out, or drawing attention to itself, a bit too attractive perhaps, like that one over there, for me to . . . I'm afraid it's going to fall out, I'm afraid it's too noticeable, I can't concentrate now . . . or speak . . . until . . . Excuse me. I must just put it back in the right place. There. It doesn't stand out now. It *was* going to fall, wasn't it? Well, maybe I'm exaggerating. I get a bit stressed out with all these books to keep in order, and at the same time it calms me down being here. I'll tell you, I'm not ashamed, the library works like an anesthetic for my hang-ups. Because when I first arrived in his town, I was in a terrible state. I'd just left Paris. I get here, in the depths of the provinces, I settle in. Or rather *we* settle in. Because I didn't come alone, you see. I wouldn't have dreamed of coming on my own to a town like this. I agreed to the move, because I made the mistake of falling in love. Big mistake. I can't understand the perennial fascination people nowadays have with love. It's a waste of time, it's a childish, tiring, stupid way of upsetting yourself. Have you ever noticed what people look like when they're in love? They look either ill or stupid. Some of them are so far gone they break out in spots or they develop tics. Well, let me tell you, I won't ever fall for it again. Because the man I came here with, the man for whom I'd given up the top-class cultural, social and professional life I had in Paris, this man, who I thought was intelligent, don't tell my colleagues, this man went off one fine day with a woman who's an engineer at the nuclear power station. I've never fallen that low. No, don't try to cheer me up. Anyway, life on earth is all down to a genetic accident, plus the obscene determination of our ancestors to reproduce themselves in the worst conditions. Take the Black Death, 1348: bang, a third of the European population wiped out. After that, for decades, people went on drawing death's heads on walls, so traumatized they were. But they went on reproducing just the same, primates that we are. Arthur (that was his name, Arthur) was my version of the Black Death, he ruined my life. So then I got a job here. At first they sent me to Life Sciences. Not that I was interested in it. I just got, pardon my language, the shitty job nobody else wanted. A very downmarket section, if you like. I stayed there three years. Then they moved me to Geography. And ever since, I've been hoping to get to my favorite section, History. But I don't think I'll ever make it. Too bad, I'll just have to be philosophical about it. All that by way of saying that after the Black Death, I was in a terrible state. Books were what saved me. I was so ashamed: imagine having been in love with a man who could find a nuclear bureaucrat charming, how uncivilized is that? Since that episode, I've given up for good any thoughts of romance or even desire. Because if a desire takes hold of you, it's dangerous, very dangerous. Watch out. I don't know what *you* do to keep going every day, but what I do is recharge my batteries here in my basement. Even though it isn't a very interesting job. If indeed there are any interesting jobs in this profession. Still, some people have better perches than me. Because a library works according to a strict hierarchy. Readers may not realize it, but we're all subject to a pitiless ranking. At the top, in his office, the Head Librarian. He comes from a top university, he decides about major acquisitions, he has his own parking space, he gets to meet writers. Then come the state-appointed librarians, category one civil servants: they're all snobs, married women with families, they're the ones who've got it all, work-life balance, tra la la, you know the type. Then come the category two civil servants, the women who work the hardest, they ride bikes to work, they're not married, people like me. I say women, because nine out of ten of the staff members in libraries are women. Apart from the Head Librarian at the top of the pyramid, the only men who work here are doing inferior jobs, like shifting books, or they're technicians, or security. I have dealings with some of them, but only to give them instructions. Anyway the women who see the most of the men in the library are the lowest-grade workers. I'm just above them, but lower down than the qualified staff. I'm in between, middle of the scale. Well, in the basement actually. Obviously, as you can see, I'm a victim of this hierarchy. But what can I do? I don't dare start a rebellion all on my own, and I don't get along with my colleagues. What could I talk about with women who go to karaoke bars in winter and museums in summer? Not for me. And anyway, to make any impression on this longstanding hierarchy, you'd have to start by making a fuss and there you go, that would stress me out. So I stay in my basement, being humiliated. Because it works between sections as well. Not all the classifications are equal. On paper, of course they are, but oh no, not in real life. French Literature and History: they're the blue-blood aristocracy, the nobles at the royal court. And on the same level you have the high society of Philosophy and Religion. Then come the minor gentry in Foreign Languages; with perhaps a bit ahead of them Economics and Social Science: they're the law lords, the legal aristocracy. Just below them, you get the bourgeoisie of periodicals and magazines: all mouth and no action. Alongside that, there's the impregnable citadel of the Children's section—let's call it the lower clergy. Not to mention, because I won't, the open shelves with C.D.s and D.V.D.s, they're the *nouveaux riches*. But *even* lower down, comes the proletariat: Science, Geography, I.T., practical books, dictionaries, travel guides. Yes. Because without their wretched user manuals on how to do Excel spreadsheets, without their thrillers and handbooks on "Writing your C.V.," do you think they'd ever get any readers into the library? Never. But it's always the same, the lower classes, who make it possible for the upper classes to hang on to their privileges, never get any consideration from the nobles. Just taxes and more taxes. Because the ranking in people's heads gets reflected on the bookshelves. Budgets for buying new books are limited, and the aristos get first pick. Us, the little folk, we come last. Crumbs from their table. It drives me crazy. Archaic, irrational . . . someone like me . . . In a basement like this . . . what was the point of guillotining Louis XVI if you still end up with everyone looking down on you? Yes, they do, they look down on me, they don't appreciate me at my true value. Upstairs, they know I didn't get to be a teacher, and they laugh at me. Even the storemen laugh, I know it. My colleague on History, she's always in late, she leaves all the worst jobs to me, she doesn't like me, and the bosses won't even let me give an opinion. But I know lots of things, I could tell them how to do *their* jobs. One day, for instance, I allowed myself to make a little remark. Since I love Maupassant, I pointed out that the only books of his in the Literature section were his bestsellers: *Boule de Suif, Bel-Ami, Le Horla*. But all his other short stories and books, *Strong as Death, Mont-Oriol*, you can't find them at all, impossible. Same thing for Simone de Beauvoir. Everyone thinks she just wrote *The Second Sex*. Well, she wrote some other great books, excellent novels, but you won't find them up there. So I pointed out to the woman in charge of the ground floor that it was pointless buying bad translations of novels from Uzbekistan that nobody borrows unless you had bought up all the books and novels by Beauvoir and Maupassant, and you know what? She just laughed in my face. Yes, she laughed in my face. A crime against culture, that's what it was. Took me weeks to get over that. Especially since, you may not realize this, it took a really, really big effort to pluck up the courage to go and make that comment. Because I absolutely hate drawing attention to myself, I'm not a natural rebel. But when, for once, I just took a small liberty, if you'd seen how she reacted, oh, it was a crime. I need to sit down, here, in Martin's armchair. Forgive me. I always sit here when something comes over me. It makes me feel better. I like this chair, it's comfy. No it's not his special place, it's just the one I'd *like* him to sit in, if he wanted to. But he always sits on his upright chair. Nothing distracts him from his studies. He's a serious student, and that's fine. So I sit down here, on my own, on these big fat cushions. When there's nobody in here, I can even read a book. One of my favorite authors, you've already gathered that, is Guy de Maupassant. Now there's a man for you. Just imagine, he wrote two hundred and ninety short stories and seven novels in ten years. And then on Sundays, he went rowing on the Seine. A real force of nature, eh? He must have had terrific biceps and been fantastically intelligent. What a man, Maupassant, and he was a poet too. He started off by writing verse. I love his style. I have to admit, he was helped a lot by Flaubert in his youth, Flaubert was like a father to him. In Maupassant's stories you often find the expression *engourdissement*—"numbness." Not a word you see often today. But it's a good word to describe the exalted state of the soul, "numbness." This armchair's so comfy, I could almost go to sleep here, this is where you should have slept last night. Personally, I prefer early Maupassant to late Maupassant. Because his later novels are a bit sentimental, I have to say. He'd left the Naval Ministry where he was a civil servant and he'd started to be a successful writer. But going around to salons and society hostesses, not all of them very reputable, prancing around, making money, that spoiled him. With his royalties, he bought a sailing boat, a Mediterranean yacht. Big mistake. The beginning of the end. Sailing's no good to anyone, whereas rowing is excellent for keeping fit. He started to fall ill, and he died at forty-three. And here, in this library, we don't even have his complete works. How shameful is that? Whereas Balzac, who was a mass-production writer, someone who pissed out prose, of course they've got the whole collection. *The Human Comedy*, oh, come on, the biggest confidence trick of the century. Balzac wrote to pay off his debts, everyone knows that. Sometimes he put together some unpublished texts, changed the title, added a couple of chapters, and Bob's your uncle, off to the printers. I can't stand that sort of thing. And because I made that humble little remark, they'll never let me run the History section or even Literature, I'm sure of it. But they're wrong, wrong, wrong. Yes, O.K., it's not as bad as all that. I'd rather be down here peacefully than have to spend my whole time working alongside the snobs upstairs. When I see the kind of books they have to put on display every day. The books that get published these days, well there's a bit of everything, but generally they're not worth reading. And if you spend your time with bad books, it doesn't improve your intelligence. So no surprises there. Have you never thought about it? What kind of literature is going to be produced in a society where there are no wars or epidemics or revolutions? I'll tell you what: badly written novels about nice girls and boys falling in love, who make each other suffer without meaning to, and spend all their time crying and saying they're sorry. Ridiculous. You should never say you're sorry. By the way, I like you, because just now, when you were lying there fast asleep between the bookcases 930 and 940, although it's absolutely against the rules, I didn't have to listen to a lot of apologies from you. On the contrary, you started shouting at me, very healthy. People apologize too much, everyone's afraid of giving offense and it leads to literature being written for babies. Lowbrow trash. That's not the way to become an adult. In September, when the autumn books come out, I see all these stupid titles invading the bookshops, and a few months later they're on the scrap heap. All the hundreds of books pouring off the presses, ninety-nine percent of them they'd do better to use the paper for wrapping takeaways. And for libraries, it's a disaster. The worst ones are the books on instant history, current affairs: no sooner commissioned than written, printed, televised, bought, remaindered, then taken off the shelves and pulped. The publishers ought to put a sell-by date on them, because they're just consumer goods. No really, the annual crop of autumn books is not my cup of tea. But every September I have to go upstairs to help the duchesses out. I obey. I can't let them down, after all. The readers besiege us every day for the latest books they've heard about the night before on the radio. They want them to be on the shelves right away. You have to resist, play for time. From all the just-published autumn books you have to select the handful worthy of gracing our shelves. It's a Herculean task. And harassing. And it doesn't really get done nowadays, no. Because I'm one of those people—although this attitude of mine has been sacrificed on the altar of cultural democratization—I'm one of those who think that it ought to be a sign of recognition for a book to be bought by a library. A distinction. An honor. And that it's up to the librarian to contribute something to the reader's culture by making a selection from the floods of new books. You have to defend yourself. These soppy sentimental novels ought to be cut out, that's what I say to Monsieur Pratier, cut right into the fat. I get along fine with Monsieur Pratier, he's my butcher, Gustave Pratier. No snobbery about him, no messing around. The same way a butcher carves up a carcass to bring out the best cuts of meat, you have to be prepared to get rid of the surplus. No more fat. No pity for bad books. When in doubt, chuck it out, that's my motto. But that kind of attitude is finished, over, I'm from the old school now. When you come into this library, what's the first thing you see? Kids wet behind the ears in front of the comic book shelves. And alongside them, Music. Just behind that, D.V.D.s, that's where cultural democracy has got us. It's not a library anymore, with silence reigning over shelves full of intelligence, it's a rec center where people come to amuse themselves. At the Ministry of Culture they lap it up, and on high the Head Librarian is perfectly happy. But you know what, Monsieur le Ministre, I've heard all your arguments: make the *médiathèque* a place of pleasure and conviviality in the very heart of the town. Make it less intimidating to go into a library. Blend culture and pleasure so that culture becomes pleasurable—and so on and so on. But it's phony, all that, it's a lie, it's manipulation. Because culture *isn't* the same thing as pleasure. Culture calls for a permanent effort by the individual to escape the vile condition of an under-civilized primate. Look what they do, they just borrow D.V.D.s, nothing but D.V.D.s. Do they even want to learn a little bit of truth about the world? No, they want to be entertained and distracted, and the zombies don't even remove their earphones. They hold out their reader's card at the lending desk just like they'd hold out a bank card to the cashier at the supermarket. If by any chance you suggest something to read, they look down at you as if they're from some superior planet. And these are the people we have to make the effort for? They just want to borrow D.V.D.s. Don't get me wrong, I have nothing against the movies, I like going to the movies on a date, not that it happens very often these days, but I appreciate it, especially if the date is well dressed and has sideburns. Arthur had sideburns, that's what undid me, but that has nothing to do with culture. In the evening they watch their D.V.D.s and I sit alone in front of the T.V., it's enough to make you weep . . . The fact is, Monsieur le Ministre, that you keep them entertained because you're afraid of them. Noise, noise, noise, never the silence of the book. We ought to react, do something, the minister is deceiving you, you young folk, he knows perfectly well that people don't begin to foster thoughts of revolution when their ears are bombarded by noise, but in the murmuring silence of reading to oneself. But it's too late now. Our shelves are already retreating under their battering rams. Before long they'll create an even deeper level for me, a cellar, and on the ground floor they'll open a café. And on this level, why not a night club while they're at it? That would really bring in the crowds, Monsieur le Ministre. Just one more step to take: develop the high-tech, expand the *videothèque*, and soon the *médiathèque* will be a *discothèque*, it's bound to happen! Ah, no, what am I saying, it's impossible, I'll never let it come to that. Forgive me if I'm getting worked up, but it's tough being in the minority. I feel like the Maginot Line of public reading. I feel so lonely sometimes, I don't know whether you understand what I'm saying. I doubt it. I'd really like to share all this with Martin. I don't know what his political opinions are. I know so little about him. The only time we had a more personal exchange, what you might call a conversation, was one Tuesday in winter. I was at my desk. He was sitting at a table, where he'd been working for about half an hour. It was quiet. The sky was gray. I didn't have any coffee left. Then suddenly Martin put the cap back on his pen, closed his book, stood up and walked over to me, with his calm movements and his long legs. I saw him coming, I looked up at him (not too fast, not to let him think I had been waiting for him), he stopped at my desk, leaned forward slightly (I wonder why, perhaps he thinks I'm deaf), I could see his shirt close up, light-blue stripes, I even picked up a hint of aftershave, a very subtle one, he was right there and he asked, oh nothing much, but so politely put, and anyway it was *me* he asked, even though that morning my History colleague was there, in his soft voice he said: "Excuse me, Madame, but would it be possible to have a little more light?" I had the chance. There he was, standing at my desk. I needed to say something to make him register my existence, to find out something about him, to tell him something about me, and hear him speak again, since for once he was looking at me. So I said: "I can put the overhead strip lighting on, but it makes a buzz." I threw out this remark to test his taste a bit, to start a conversation—agreed it wasn't very great, but he should have guessed I was flustered. But he just answered: "Oh that doesn't matter, but please, I would prefer more light." And he went back to his seat. I was a bit disappointed. I've often thought about it since. I replay the scene in my head. I ask myself what I should have replied, what he would have said in return, and so on. Don't take this the wrong way, but it's a pity it was you and not Martin that got locked in my basement. If it had been Martin, we could have had highly intellectual conversations, lasting hours and hours, even if it meant ending up exhausted, drained, worn out . . . We would have had a really intelligent exchange. Well, that's not how it worked out. Since that brief conversation, on a December morning, I like winter better. Before, I used to dread it. Winter, you know, is always a bit special. During the really cold months, the library fills up with a lot of desperate people: the homeless, families with young children, dropouts with their plastic bags, it's a real refugee center. You see them feeling awkward, because they don't really know what to do in the reading room, but at home it's miserable and freezing cold. So our big attraction, on cold days, isn't our incunabula, or our evening lecture program, nooooo . . . it's our central heating. Nice, reliable, comfortable central heating, November to April. It's our gas supply that draws in these wretched masses. They're not really readers. They wander around. To the magazine corner, then to Literature. They come down here so as not to be noticed. They pretend to read. They don't make a noise, they just look for some little spot and hope everyone will forget about them. Sometimes, if they land in an armchair, they drop off to sleep, poor things. I do feel a lot of sympathy for them. I call them the "central heating refugees." Sometimes, like with you, I offer them some coffee. Only if they look clean. There are limits. My little refugees all disappear in the spring. Their places are taken by students stressed out about their exams. Not the same atmosphere. Much noisier. They come with their pals to revise their lecture notes and commandeer my tables. I have to keep a close eye on them and often ask them to be quiet. Not speaking when you're in a group is unnatural, but it's part of learning to be civilized. Except for me. For me, not speaking comes naturally. Well, O.K., today it's different, because you're here, but otherwise, as a rule, I keep my mouth shut. Apart from the students, spring is usually a pretty quiet season. I get bored here with all my shelf marks in the same place. It gets to me in the end.

Sometimes the readers think we're being grumpy toward them. You have to understand us: who'd choose to come and shut themselves up under these neon lights and inside these plasterboard walls when the sun's just starting to send out the first timid rays of warmth and the grass is greening under the wind at lambing time, eh? I ask you. Only damned souls like us, the captives of culture, locked in our silo, who else would let themselves be locked in like this? You can't think how boring it can get. You fill out order slips, the students are revising, I peer up at the blue sky through the windows and think of Martin. In spring, I see much less of him. Not that I'm jealous, that's not the way I am, but something tells me he's with someone. With that lovely neck of his. It would disappoint me if a man as clever as Martin were to be in love. But you have to be prepared for anything. Sometimes I see him chatting with girls. With that beautiful neck . . . But I don't have time to mope, because in summer, the library is full to bursting. Different readers, people on vacation passing through, research students, and lots of little old men. I like summer. I talk to the regulars, people like you, nice people, a bit shy but nice. They all have their favorite subjects. There's this one reader, Monsieur Billot, I'm sure you know him, he always wears a red waistcoat, and he's obsessive. He cuts up photocopies of newspaper articles and puts them in huge scrapbooks, all about dog bites or fairground accidents. Actually we've got plenty of people with obsessions, not to mention half a dozen people fixated on Ancient Egypt. Yes, you're right, it is striking. Ancient Egypt exerts a fascination over the weak-minded, I've seen it several times in my career. You wouldn't believe the number of unemployed, or pensioners, handicapped people or welfare recipients that you get in the library in summer. They come here as a sort of exercise, it's kind of like jogging or walking the dog. They need something to do. Some of them mix it up: they go to the law courts on Tuesdays and Thursdays, when the preliminary hearings are held, and on Wednesdays and Fridays they come to the municipal library. Ah, it's the other way around, is it? If you say so. Well, you get your entertainment where you can. People can be lonely, terribly lonely. Reading's an excuse. A pretext. What they're looking for here is something to hang on to. If you don't believe me, how come you don't even want to go home at night? Who would come and shut themselves up in this basement if they were of sound mind? Yes, go on, admit it, you're a bit borderline yourself. Well, anyway, libraries do attract crazy people. Especially in summer. Of course, if you closed the libraries during summer vacation, you wouldn't see them. No more lunatics, poor people, children on their own, students who've failed their exams, no more little old men, no more culture and no more humanity. When I think that some mayors dare to close their libraries in August. Just to cut down on costs. Barbaric. Think of it: when the town's sweltering in the heat, the shops are all closed, the swimming pools are full, people's purses are empty, their pay's too low, and they're brooding over their problems in the shade, with the tar melting on the road, the house of culture could be opening its arms to all those children lost in an ocean of urban idiocy, but no, his highness the Mayor has closed the library. The bastard. What's the little old pensioner going to do in August? I'll tell you: he gets up on Tuesday morning, he takes the only bus of the day, and he toddles along slowly to the entrance of the library, because for twenty-four hours he's been looking forward to a nice long day spent in an air-conditioned reading room, leafing through his favorite newspapers, and then like a stab in the back, or Napoleon's *coup d'etat*, my poor little pensioner sees the criminal notice on the door:

Closed until September. And then Durkheim is surprised there are more suicides in summer. It's so sad. Nothing is sadder than an empty library. I mean a library that's open, but with no readers. It can happen, though, in any season. And there we sit, like Uncle Scrooge McDuck on his hoard of gold. Because for all that I'm being a bit hard on you, what would we actually do if there weren't any readers? Some of my colleagues upstairs, in their huge ground floor space, with their big windows and perfectly ordered shelves, they're so comfortable sitting there alongside their coffee machines, that they actually talk out loud about how nice it would be in a library without readers. Like some teachers dream of a school with no pupils. But what would be the point of us then? Oh, yes, it would be in perfect order. A mathematical masterpiece, really shipshape, our library. But what would be the point if nobody came along to disturb it? I like it when a new reader comes down the stairs into my cellar, it makes a change. I always look up to see who it is. Every time I hear someone coming down the stairs, I get palpitations. Sort of a funny turn. Not just for Martin, because it happens when he's already down here, but every time I hear a reader's footsteps it's as if I'm waiting, hoping, how shall I put it? Well, yes, for something to happen. It's stupid, I know, but I can't help it. Every reader that appears starts it up again, I get palpitations. Then afterward, I always feel upset with myself. Because, obviously, the reader arrives, sits down, reads a book, and goes away. That's all. So what's the big deal? Nobody's asked me anything, nothing's happened. But really that's all I *do* want, to be asked a question, to be disturbed, just a bit. Even you, for instance, you come here every other day, but you've never done that. Why not? You know, in my job, there's nothing more exciting, that makes you feel more wanted, than to be able to size up the person in front of you, guess what they're after, find the book they need on the shelves and bring the two together. Book and reader, if they meet up at the right moment in a person's life, it can make sparks fly, set you alight, change your life. It can, I promise you. I don't know if you can understand that, perhaps it's beyond you. Well of course, in the Geography section, my ambitions are very limited. I only occasionally have that happen here. I just adapt. But I'm a limited person myself, modest and humble. Any human being who has even a smidgeon of culture must one day take stock of their total impotence. In my case, the older I get, the more aware I become of my limits. The older I get, the chances of Martin ever looking at me are shrinking all the time. I know it. Every day spent here takes me a step nearer the grave. Soon it will be over. Not very nice for a man, but for a woman it's even worse. That depresses me. The only thing that consoles me is to be surrounded by people as depressed as I am. The readers down here, they're *seriously* depressed and that cheers me up. You yourself for instance, if I can put this politely, you don't exactly look like a bundle of laughs. No, don't pretend, I can see right through you. You're sad, and lonely. But if you didn't come in here, it'd be worse. No, don't argue, you're absolutely right to come here. You should never just sit around moping at home. When your family's abandoned you, you haven't got any friends, you think you're awful, worthless, nothing, books are a great help. Just think about it: what can make human beings suffer more than awareness of their limits? I don't mean fear of death, I mean our suffering at realizing our intelligence is limited. But when we go into a library and look at all those bookcases stretching into the distance, what descends on our soul, if not grace? Spiritually, we can at last fill the terrible emptiness that makes us just worms creeping on this earth. Those endless bookshelves reflect back to us an ideal image, the image of the full range of the human mind. Then all the paths are made plain, everything's newly created once more, and we move closer to a mystical vision of Abundance. The inexhaustible milk of human culture, right here, within our reach. Help yourself, it's free. Borrow, because as much as accumulation of material things impoverishes the soul, cultural abundance enriches it. My culture doesn't stop where someone else's begins. In fact, the library is the place where the greatest solidarity between humans takes place. Humanity, in its most depressing and suffering state, the most beautiful humanity there is, actually, the sinners, the unemployed, the cold weather refugees, they're all around me here. Knock and it shall be opened to you, ask and you shall be served . . . What? You're laughing? Oh good grief, for once I was being serious, and I got carried away again. But you're right, let me put it more clearly. So you can understand, I'll tell you who typically never sets foot here: a rich white man between the ages of thirty-five and fifty. Why? Because in that age group, he's part of the barbaric ruling class. Monsieur doesn't make use of public services. You'll never see Monsieur on a bus. Monsieur doesn't need to share with other people, because Monsieur owns things. It's a long time now since Monsieur's madame went to borrow some eggs from the neighbor. Because for Mother's Day, she got a three-speed mixer, and if Monsieur cares to read a book, he buys it. But in any case, reading is already an act of weakness. Monsieur has purchasing power. A house. Two cars. Monsieur doesn't have the time. He has a subscription to a sports club. Does he ever think about the facilities provided by his local council? No, he thinks he's all-powerful, a self-made man, what an ass. Life isn't preprogrammed like a washing machine. Just wait till he gets a tumor in some corner of his brain, or loses his job, or his wife cheats on him, or his tax returns get inspected. Or all four at once. Then you'll see him turning up, tail between his legs. Who's sorry now? His telephone's stopped ringing. Suddenly, he has all the time in the world. So he'll come and start flipping through the pages of the newspapers and realize he doesn't know anything about public affairs—he'll be amazed at our new system that lets you borrow books for six weeks at a time, renewable once. His wife will leave him, he'll become obsessive or depressed, he'll start bowling, and even become a pedestrian. He'll be one of us. But it will have taken all those body-blows from life for him to understand that the library, that building he used to go past with utter indifference, doesn't hold a lot of dead books, no, it's the beating heart of the Great Consolation. I'd go further. What do you think all this represents, the welcoming arms of the bookshelves, the soft carpets underfoot, the restful semi-silence, the warm temperature, the discreet and benevolent supervision? You can't guess? Don't be afraid to say what you think. Let me remind you, I'm completely neutral toward you, and anything we say in this room won't go beyond these four walls. You still don't get it? But it's obvious. Going into the library is nothing more or less than getting back onto your mommy's lap. Yes, like Mommy, the library gives you a magic kiss and everything's better. Love life in ruins? Hate everyone? Despair over the state of the planet? Headache? Insomnia? Indigestion? Corns? I can tell you, there's nothing the library can't cure. In fact, the therapists send us agoraphobics because they know that here their patients will meet a crowd of people who are peaceful, at one with the rest of humanity: the students revising around tables they share without any fuss, the grandfathers quietly reading, the well-behaved children, a constant mixture of cerebral essences, floating around in the rational stratification of ideas provided by the Dewey Decimal System. Yes, this vision of humanity raises us onto a higher plane. Ah, Martin . . . Oh, what are you doing now? No, don't sit there, that's my desk. I didn't go to all the trouble of doing the internal

exams at the age of forty to end up without a
desk of my own. This is my place. This is where
I sit to select, classify, answer queries, catalog,
listen and occasionally—as I told you—give
advice. If people ask me nicely. Now, where's my
watch gone? Here's something else. My jewelry.
Some earrings. I hide them in a drawer and I put
them on discreetly when I see Martin arrive. You
don't catch flies with vinegar, as my mother
would say. Poor woman: she's never read a book
in her life, but on that subject she's a walking
encyclopedia. And if I'd listened to her, I would
have kept a closer eye on the Black Death and the
radioactive fallout from the nuclear power station. She did warn me, my mother. Watch out,
she said. One never does watch out enough. You
trust people, you go with the flow, you drop off
to sleep, and oops, there you are in a basement
all night. I'm teasing you. You're lucky it was
a week night, or you might have spent the whole
weekend in here, starving to death. Oh, here's my
watch. Excuse me, I have to do a few things, we'll

be opening soon. It's not all set up yet. The trolleys have to be emptied, it all has to look neat and tidy. Even if, between ourselves, most people have no idea of all I've been telling you, what goes on here. Most readers don't come for the good of their soul. Some of them don't come to borrow books, or to work, not even to read . . . No, don't pretend you don't know, it happens at any age: I mean picking people up. No, don't look so surprised, you hypocrite. I'm not criticizing you. It's a game two can play, women are just as likely to be doing it as men. I don't know what your method is. But I've seen all sorts of tactics. I've seen people collect a pile of books and leave them all over a table to give an idea of their taste and their personality, and wait to see what kind of fish will bite. I've seen others who are more daring—they make a point of ostentatiously reading sex manuals. Shelf mark 306.7, surefire magnet for boys, and the people who work here aren't made of stone. I know colleagues who've found notes on the desk, like: "I'm sitting in the third row down, and I'll buy you a coffee if you can get a break." Then there are the real prima donnas, who turn up in skimpy tops and short skirts even when the air conditioning is on, they jump up every ten minutes, they walk between the bookshelves, click-clack with their heels, wiggling their bottoms, the boys opposite are beside themselves, they try to concentrate, but no, it's just impossible. So they shoot glances from one table to another, they get up, go out for a smoke and there you are. Well, people have to have a bit of fun. Because books in themselves aren't sexy, they're silent, cold, off-putting. At night, when the library's empty, it's really scary. Last night you were scared, weren't you, and cold, well of course, that's normal. Be honest, these dreaded books impress us, don't they? Even me, do you think I've got things under control here? Not at all, I'm their slave. If they're in the wrong order, they start shouting at me, and I have to hurry along like a servant to put them right, get them into the proper shelf. But I'm free, aren't I, to do what I like? If I wanted to push a pile of books over, there's nothing to stop me. Look here we go . . . just let me get a life, why don't you? . . . O.K., O.K., it wasn't such a great idea, sorry. I can't stand it. Just seeing them all over the floor . . . Help me pick them up, I don't know what came over me then. I get these funny impulses sometimes. One day for instance, in the bathroom, I saw this graffiti: *Young man would like to meet young woman who admires Critique of Pure Reason for Kantian adventure.* There was even a cell phone number. Now don't tell the Librarian, but I wrote underneath, *Mature woman would like to meet young man who admires Critique of Dialectical Reason for Sartrean adventure.* Obviously, not everyone would get it. And nobody ever replied. Admittedly, I didn't dare put my phone number. But I don't see why I shouldn't have a bit of fun too, instead of watching the readers getting off with each other and the books stacking up. I've got a right to something, haven't I? I don't see why, since I'm neither more nor less depressed than anyone else, I should have to spend my whole life not being noticed. My whole life, down in this basement. Martin, I know perfectly well, never looks at me. He's totally indifferent to me. And yet I do everything I can to make it nice here. I've had armchairs brought in, I got hold of a potted plant. You don't see many of those in libraries. Perhaps Martin doesn't like rubber plants. I don't know what I have to do to get his attention. Put a note in with his borrower's slip? I can't offer him a bunch of flowers! Such a lovely neck . . . No, never, he never so much as looks at me. He just sits there reading his old history books, that really gets me. I ought to go up to him, I really feel this, I should say, Martin, it's so stupid reading all those books. Don't fool yourself, how many of these wretched books do you think you know? Go on, you've got plenty of intelligence, so let's say you

read two books a week, for fifty years. In your life-
time, you'll have read how many? Five thousand?
That's nothing. Nothing at all, compared to what
we have here: two hundred and fifty thousand,
seven hundred different books. And in the
National Library, they've got fourteen million.
We're just cockroaches. So we'd do better to have
a bit of fun, look at each other, talk and reproduce, don't you think? If you like, we can go to
Versailles, together, any time at all, we can go
wherever you want to go, to some beach somewhere, I'll be your Pompadour and we'll love
each other until the end of love, hand in hand,
we'll gaze at the sea, the sea that begins and
ceases and then again begins, the pounding of the
surf, the flow of water, the flow of light coming in
new every day, fresh surges from the deep, the tide
will carry us off, and the flow of paper, every year
fifty thousand new titles, fifty thousand books
fighting for the chance to come swell our groan-
ing bookshelves, and every year they make me
more aware of my limited span, my old age and

my insignificance. Yes. It's all an illusion, a massive illusion. You never feel so miserable as in a library. You can bow down in front of books all you like, try to understand, read and reread them, but there's no hope. You know this perfectly well. Books can't do anything for us. They will always win out. In fact, if you don't keep trying to hold the lid down on them, they'll kill us all, the damn things. They have their own logic. Remember, last month? There was an armchair here and four reader's seats. All gone. Replaced by two bookcases made of particleboard, for shelf mark 960. The counterrevolution is under way. We have to do something. Their aim is the elimination of all readers from the library. I can see the books planning it. They hold meetings, they pile up in towers, they barricade themselves in the stores, and once they've gathered enough strength, they charge. With the help of some of the librarians, the aristos on the staff, they're getting the best places, bit by bit. The readers step back, stumble, resist a little, but gradually get pushed out, they're in the way, human beings are in the way, and they know it. So, in the end, they throw up their hands and leave. That's it. *Finito*, "The dead eat up the living" as the old saying goes. I'll tell you how it works. The library is the arena where every day the Homeric battle between books and readers begins. In this struggle, the librarians are the referees. In this arena, they have a part to play. Either they're cowards and take the side of the mountain of books, or they bravely help the worried reader. And in this fight, you have to let your conscience be your guide. But librarians aren't automatically on the side of the humans, don't be fooled. You don't realize, but you're a flock of sheep in our hands, you think you're gamboling around free as air, but there are wolves everywhere lying in wait for you, cyclops, sirens, naked nymphs, oh, the pity of it . . . A barricade only has two sides and I know which side I'm on, comrade. I'm here to help the poor, depressed, thirsty reader faced with the crushing prestige of the Army of Books. You haven't noticed, because I keep myself to myself, but I'm on your side and always have been. On the side of the pedestrians, the bowlers, the regulars. With my shelf marks 900 and 910. Some people have chosen the other side, the duchesses up there at 200 and 800. My class enemies. Look out, Lady, look out! I see them, the thought police of the library, I've seen the way they talk to the readers. They hit them over the head with "You must read *this*, or *that*." They decide what's "well-written" and what isn't, they're like statues of the *Commendatore* for French literature. They say that everyone must have access to Literature with a big "L," then they put up this huge monument—the Classics—and it demands sacrificial victims every day, new flesh, fresh blood. With the duchesses, you're never on the right foot, never. They're the cultural cops. If you set foot in their precinct, hesitating, a bit unsure of yourself, you're afraid they'll call you over. "Hey, you. Yes, you! Show me your classics please. Hmm. Yes, very unsatisfactory, lots of gaps there. How long is it since you opened a book by Balzac? Hmm. Occupation? Do you have a full-time job? Oh well, you have no excuse. I'd be ashamed if I were you. What's that book in the bag? Open it, please. Oh, I see, very interesting. Easy reading. Airport book. Glossy cover. Badly written. Trash! And you plan on staying sometime in this cultural state, do you? You'll have to be taken in hand. I'm recommending a set of eighteenth-century classics for you, for ten months. Don't argue, you have no choice. Report back to me after that. No, leave this book here, please. And don't let me catch you again. Right, on your way now." The brutes. I would never, ever let myself say things like that. Attacking the readers that way. Not even Martin, no. Anyway, I'll tell you this, it doesn't work. It doesn't work any longer. On the contrary, you need kindness, more kindness, always more kindness. I see them come in here, the young kids from technical school, apprentices, the children who need study support. The first time, they come in groups, no way are they going to set foot in the library on their own. They come in with their friends, they make a lot of noise. As if they're trying it on to show they're not intimidated, but of course they are, poor things, they're terrorized. They shiver as they enter the arena, they know the books aren't on their side. When you've always been useless at school, thousands of books all gathered together in one place are scary, humiliating, for a man they're castrating— well, that's another story. So, now my little flock settles down. That's when you have to go over to them with a big smile and welcome them. They've got a project to do for school. I bring them some books. They whisper to each other, they don't sit still. The regulars give them dirty looks, but it's not too bad. Then some of them come back. They start to know their way around.

They read pretty useless books, but at least they're reading. It can take months, this kindness offensive. We know we've won when they come back all on their own. That's when they feel at home, they're accepted, they're reassured. They have a right to be here. "School sometimes makes mistakes, and the library can put them right," that's what Eugène Morel said. Ah . . . Eugène. Ah . . . Martin. Yes, indeed, you can accomplish great things if you're a librarian. That's why I really can't understand why Martin is so indifferent toward me. O.K., I didn't get the right grades for the teaching certificate, but still, I'm not so bad, am I? Answer, please. What does this kid want? To meet an I.T. manageress? A woman who puts the bills in A.T.M.s? A woman who sells private swimming pools? A nuclear power station engineer? No, I really don't get it. Here I am doing a useful, interesting and brave job, one that calls for a whole lot of qualities. When they bring a book back: "Yes, I liked that one too, did you?" Point out another they might like. Gently ease them away from the bestseller shelves. Apply emotional tactics. Agreed, they don't always work. I may not be that good at it. But I could say in my defense that it all depends on what's gone before. At the very beginning. Everything depends on the very first days, the first time someone walks over the threshold. That's when it starts. The beginnings of civilization. Birth. The primal scene. Before that, frankly, the reader is a virgin. Yes, a virgin. And I like to see people losing their library cherry. Oh well, of course, if the first time is a fiasco, it'll be hard to carry on. Very hard. If the librarian comes charging at you like a bull, no kindness, no foreplay, that's it. You'll never come back. Divorced from culture. Lifelong abstinence. Don't wriggle around in your seat like that, I'm not going to bite you. Be patient, only a quarter of an hour until opening time. There are plenty of ways to humiliate the virgin reader, to abuse or terrorize him or her. Those counter-revolutionaries upstairs, they know all about that. The first tactic is the Dewey decimal classification. What a perverse invention, an instrument of torture. Does anyone understand why it jumps from 300 to 500, leaving out 400? Stupid, anarchic, mega-moronic. The Dewey system is a secret code invented by the Axis of Evil that binds books and librarians together in order to scare the reader off. It's terrifying, the Dewey system. Totally inhibiting. Everything goes into it, like a mincer. Your vacations, your house, your tastes, your furniture, just everything. There's even a classification for sexuality—and plenty of different shelf marks for all the complications. No, sorry, we don't have that down here, it's upstairs. "Reserve Section." I'm telling you, if no one stops them, the people on the ground floor will end up putting a shelf mark on all of us; my refugees, my unemployed, my little old men, everyone, shelf marked. We mustn't let them get away with it. They're *perverts*. Their supreme sin is to set up a system where the books are all in the stacks and you have to fill out a request slip. You go into a library, but instead of looking at the books, being able to pull them out and handle them and borrow when you want . . . no, they shut them up in stacks, in a big cold warehouse. As if they were too precious to be touched. And how do you get hold of books that are hidden? You have to fill out this little slip, very clearly, and humbly present it at the desk. It drives me nuts, this antiquated way of doing things. Twenty minutes later, or even half an hour, they deign to bring you your book, and they ask you for your surname, please, now your first name. It's as if they were stripping you naked in front of everyone. And no more than three books at a time, blah blah blah. The assault course is scattered with obstacles and ambushes, like red-hot brands to mark the first-time visitor. You have to know which book to order, so you have to consult the catalog, and good luck to you if you aren't familiar with its little ways. Then you fill out your "little slip." Then you have to wait. And waiting already sets you up for humiliation. Your desire for the book gets blunted, and by the time the book arrives the reader has gathered that nobody cares about his enthusiasm. They've arranged everything it takes to put people off for life, to cause immense frustration. Of course, after that, I can't pick up the pieces, the damage has been done. Not to mention that a traumatic system like this leads to the development of library neurosis, repression on a grand scale, and before you know it, outbreaks of sex attacks and cultural violence, I don't have to draw a diagram, do I? Oh, hear that noise? They're winding the blinds up. The doors will be open soon. I'd better put my earrings on, you never know. I'm going to confess something to you. About the back of his neck. No, I've had plenty of time to think about it, haven't I, so I've thought about it a lot. This other evening, I was at my desk. I had this book in my hands and I was just going to reshelve it. A solid sort of book, a hardback with a nice squared spine. And as I was putting it into place, I looked at it again, among the others. And seen from the back, this book reminded me of something, but what? And then, I kid you not, I had this revelation. It was the back of Martin's neck. Yes. Then I understood. What's the spine of a book, if not its nape? No need to look at me like that, anyone can see you don't spend your life among people and books with their backs turned on you. Well, this flash of insight just blew my mind. Now, even looking at that bookcase, I sometimes get a funny feeling . . . The worst thing is when Martin is wandering around among the books. All I have to do is get up, and pretend I've got something to sort out. I can follow him quite closely. I try to sneak along a few steps behind him. And that's when I get the most beautiful sight of all: the back of Martin's neck, a kind of synthesis, a universal résumé of Man's inviolate buttocks, wandering through hundreds of books all with *their* backsides turned toward you, and the two buttocks multiplied infinitely and magnified by the nape of Martin's neck, it makes me want to, well, I don't know what I might be capable of. But not in the Town Planning and Geography section, no, it's completely impossible. Now don't you go telling the Head Librarian that, eh? I don't want to lose my job. I'm already in their bad buttocks here, *books*, I mean, bad *books* . . . No, don't snicker, as if I were the only one with ideas like that. As if being in daily contact with our great works of literature placed an invisible and chaste veil over our age-old primitive impulses. Pardon me while I smile. You think perhaps that writers are respectable people? No, in order to write (I've thought about this one too), you have to have a sexual problem. It's obvious. Either too much libido or too little. Whichever. But writing is a sexual activity. So you see for me, in the middle of all these books, with Martin there, almost within arm's reach . . . Luckily there are two thousand years of civilization behind me, and the rubber plant between us, otherwise . . . What was I saying? Oh yes, writing is a sexual activity. You don't shut yourself up for ten hours a day to write if everything in your life is absolutely hunky-dory. Writing only happens when something's wrong. If everyone on earth was happy, they wouldn't write anything except recipes and postcards, and there wouldn't be any books, or literature, or libraries. It would be the sign that humanity had finally dealt with all its traumas and sexual hang-ups. Because in the end that's all writers ever think about. Take Maupassant, for instance: he went insane before he died. After *Le Horla*, the critics churned out pages of stuff about how it displayed existential angst which had been there since his childhood, and a repressed dual personality, and so on and so on. Oh, give me a break! The truth is that Maupassant died from the final brain lesions resulting from a case of syphilis that wasn't properly treated. Maupassant was sexually obsessed. Remember the night he got Flaubert, plus some official, to stand witness that he could have sex with six women of the night in one hour? Away to the whorehouse, under starter's orders, and they're off! Great role model, wouldn't you say? Anyway, Maupassant said, "Bel-Ami, that's me." And *Bel-Ami* isn't a satire on the world of journalism, as they say in those textbooks for provincial schoolchildren. *Bel-Ami* isn't even a novel, it's an ode to male potency as a weapon of domination, allied to money. How exemplary is that? And what about Balzac, eh? A man who spends his time in his bathrobe, drinking cup after cup of black coffee, would you like him to marry your daughter? And Sartre? Even worse. An old satyr, and an alcoholic. He smoked, he drank whisky, and he stuffed himself with pills on top of that. If they'd offered him the Nobel Prize for substance abuse, I bet he wouldn't have turned it down. Everyone knows he wrote *Nausea* under the influence of mescaline. Simone de Beauvoir, who liked her tipple too, by the way, says she could hear him munching amphetamines while he was writing . . . Martin, now—with him it's chocolate. Sartre, you know, with his pills, by the end of the day he was deaf as a post . . . No, Martin never offers me a piece of chocolate, I suppose it's a bit too intimate. It was Sartre, and only Sartre, who forced all this free union stuff on Simone de Beauvoir, with affairs left, right and center. *She* wouldn't have minded getting married. But Sartre just thought about himself . . . Yes, there he sits, taking notes for his thesis, when all the time I could be telling him about the *ancien régime*. Louis XV for example: now *he* was a pedophile. No need to spend years doing research to learn that . . . Contingent loves and necessary loves, all that nonsense, oh, she suffered, poor Simone . . . No, Martin prefers to flirt with his blonde. Yes, there's a blonde in the picture—the other day she even dared ask me a question, oh I wasn't going to help *her*, worse than an architect . . . Nobody will say this, but take it from me—Beauvoir used to throw these jealous tantrums with Sartre, but he wouldn't budge an inch. Like Martin. Whatever I try, he never so much as looks at me . . . So when he went chasing after some other woman, Simone had to copy him. But it was because she was hurt. And I understand . . . So what am I supposed to do? Try and get off with one of the warehousemen? Bring in another rubber plant? Borrow some D.V.D.s? . . . It's pitiful. There was a lot of talk about the American, Nelson Algren, Simone had an affair with. But it was Sartre who started it. When he was in the States, the great philosopher fell for some little American tootsie. So what do you expect, poor Simone was bound to feel abandoned . . . I can see him now, Martin, chatting about Madame de Pompadour with his blonde hussy . . . So of course, being hurt, Beauvoir found herself a transatlantic oddball, look at me, I'm doing the same as

Jean-Paul. And she called herself a feminist! Oh, the heartache . . . Martin and this blonde, no it breaks my heart to imagine that he could be in love . . . And don't try to cheer me up, you can't know what it's like waiting in this basement every day for Martin to come down the stairs, it's awful. One morning they even arrived together, him and his blonde. He might even be sleeping with her. Right here, in my library! That woman . . . Then Simone de Beauvoir, with all that suffering and misery and love inside her, spent the next five years writing *The Mandarins*, five years, her best book, shelf mark FR BEA . . . But what can I do, I'm just a cockroach. Wait for Martin to arrive, then lock him in the basement one night? I'd never dare, I know that perfectly well. But why doesn't he come and ask me questions more often? Then something might finally happen . . . That's all I ask. Why does Martin just leave me alone with these damned books? Tell me, frankly, do you think a boy like him might one day actually look at me? . . . Poor old Simone and poor old me . . . No, really, I never thought culture would turn out like this. Wait, I can hear something now . . . Yes, they're opening up. You can go upstairs now and get out. I'm truly sorry for what happened. But please, don't go repeating anything I said. I feel a bit ashamed now. You mustn't take it literally. It was just, you know, a flight of fancy. It isn't always easy to stay put, you have to do what you can. You caught me unawares and sometimes in this prison, with all the books, something's got to give. Yes, some days it feels like I could die down here and nobody would notice. People don't know where the library is. They walk by without seeing me. Ungrateful bunch. I've never got a word of thanks from Martin, my refugees, my little old men, my school dunces. Once they leave here, they forget about me. I'm stuck in my basement, while the duchesses upstairs are giggling. When I get home at night, I can't even bring myself to read. And yet it all starts up again every day. I fall for it. The

Homeric struggle. Every day, I go back into the arena. Every day I say to myself: What if he doesn't come? What if all is lost? What good will it have been to put shelf marks on all these books? What good will it have been to spend my entire youth in overheated libraries? Yes, what's the point of Simone de Beauvoir and Eugène Morel if Martin doesn't come?

SOPHIE DIVRY lives in Lyon. She likes eggplants, olive oil and her mother's homemade jam. She hates cars, is a feminist and has a phobia about open doors. She likes swimming in the sea, lakes or rivers, but does not like buying a book without knowing what's inside it. *The Library of Unrequited Love* is her first novel.

SIÂN REYNOLDS is a past winner of the Scott Moncrieff Translation prize, and has translated many French writers, from Fernand Braudel to Fred Vargas. She lives in Edinburgh.

About the Type

Text set in Albertina at 11.75/16.5pt.

Albertina is a typeface designed by Chris Brand in the early 1960s. An accomplished calligrapher, Brand sought to adapt the hand-lettered forms for the age of moveable type.

Typeset by Scribe Inc., Philadelphia, Pennsylvania